This book is for you, Tess and Rory.
You are the dreams of our life story!
Love, Mom & Dad

Text copyright © 2009 by Amy Schmidt
Photographs copyright © 2009 by Ron Schmidt

Published in the United States by Random House Children's Books, a division of Random House, Inc., New York.

Random House and colophon are registered trademarks of Random House, Inc.

Visit us on the Web! www.randomhouse.com/kids

Educators and librarians, for a variety of teaching tools, visit us at
www.randomhouse.com/teachers

Library of Congress Cataloging-in-Publication Data
Schmidt, Amy.
Loose leashes / poems by Amy Schmidt ; photographs by Ron Schmidt. — 1st ed.
p. cm.
ISBN 978-0-375-85641-9 (trade) — ISBN 978-0-375-95641-6 (lib. bdg.)
1. Dogs—Juvenile poetry. 2. Children's poetry, American. 3. Dogs—Pictorial works. I. Schmidt, Ron. II. Title.
PS3619.C4453L66   2009
811'.6—dc22 2008021716

Printed in the United States of America
10 9 8 7 6 5 4 3 2

First Edition

Poems by Amy Schmidt

Loose Leashes

Photographs by Ron Schmidt

Random House ⌂ New York

Loose Leashes

My leash was loose,
So now I'm off
To see the world,
Out on my own.
Down country roads
And city streets,
In my red car,
Free and alone.
Armed with my map,
I'm going far—
Just need to learn to drive this car.

(Skedaddle)

Timber

Out among the pines
A laberjack spends his day.
Timber! A tree falls.

(Laberjack)

Grace

It would be great
If I could skate
A figure eight,
But my poor legs just won't keep straight.

It would be keen
If I was seen
To skate one clean,
But with four legs I make sixteen!

(Grace)

I Will **NOT** Go
to the Groomer

I will not go to the groomer
And won't be washed outside.
To be bathed in a public place
Is quite undignified.

I need a little privacy,
Some quiet time to think.
So if you'll kindly draw my bath,
I'll soak here in the sink.

(Honey)

Love

Can you feel my eyes upon you, melting you with my stare?
I know we're very different. We'd make an awkward pair.
But your stunning grace and beauty are far beyond compare.
I've waited here for hours. I'm starting to despair,
For every time you glance my way, you gaze into thin air.
You may not ever notice me. Sometimes love's not fair.

(Moose and Mini)

Adventurers

Rowing,
Flowing,
Downstream by boat.
Then we spy something
Small, green, and afloat!

Steering,
Nearing,
Peering. A ball!
Loud water crashing—
Look out!

Water
 f
  a
   l
    l!

(Lewie and Clark)

Sharing is always a hard thing to do,
Especially when one bone is given to two.
As they growl and pull
With all of their might,

(Pip and Squeak)

of the **Bone**

This bone tug-of-war lasts all through the night.
At sunrise they curl into one furry heap,
Their battle forgotten.
The winner is sleep.

Learning to Swim

It was sad but true.
I hadn't a clue.
I was too afraid to swim.

My poor tail would shake.
My body would quake.
My chances to learn looked slim.

I missed out on fun
Sweating in the sun.
I sat poolside sad and grim.

Enough was enough!
I had to get tough.
I needed help to begin.

I took a swim class,
Which was easy to pass,
And now I just jump right in!

(Splash)

How Do You Find a Way to Keep Cool?

How do you find a way to keep cool
  on a sticky-hot summer day?
Do you seek out a shady tree and nap the day away?
Do you slurp up lots of water?
Do you sit in front of a fan?
Do you splash around in a pool?
Do you hunt for the ice cream man?
How do *we* find a way to keep cool
  on a sticky-hot summer day?
We jump into our rubber tubes and float around the bay!

(Pa and Pea)

M O N T E

and the Demise of His Eyes

There once was a dog that could read
With amazing page-turning speed.
People thought it an act,
But it was a fact—
This dog was an uncommon breed.

One evening a strange thing occurred.
While reading, his sight became blurred.
He squinted his eyes
But was sadly surprised
To see lines blurred, word into word.

A vet claimed, "Your dog is all right.
Just weak eyes affecting his sight."
The dog got new glasses,
Began taking classes,
And now he is learning to write!

(Monte)

Surfing

With surfboard in tow, I sniff out the spot
Where the waves whirl and twirl and curl.
Down long winding paths I slowly trot.
With surfboard in tow, I sniff out the spot.
The path opens wide to the beach I have sought.
The sand leads to sea, where big waves unfurl.
With surfboard in tow, I sniff out the spot
Where the waves
whirl
and twirl
and curl.

(Woody)

Clean Dog, Smelly Dog:
A Tail of Woe

Clean means . . .
>. . . into the house
>. . . into the room
>. . . onto the bed
>. . . under the covers.

Smelly means . . .
>. . . out of the covers
>. . . off the bed
>. . . out of the room
>. . . kicked out of the house.

So what's a smelly dog to do?
Climb into the tub and get a shampoo!

(Stinky)

Anchors Aweigh

I've roamed the world aboard a ship
From sea to shining sea,
Was born and bred a salty dog.
That's been the life for me.
But now I'm searching for a place
To lay my anchor down.
Anchors aweigh . . .
Anchors aweigh . . .

I've been to the Hawaiian isles
And learned to hula dance.
I've gone up the Eiffel Tower
And found romance in France.

I've witnessed the bright
   northern lights,
Outrun a polar bear.
I've summited Mount Everest
And panted in thin air.

I've journeyed through the Amazon.
I've traveled down the Nile.
I've spent some quiet time alone
On a deserted isle.
But still I'm searching for a place
To lay my anchor down.
Anchors aweigh . . .
Anchors aweigh . . .

Land ho! A port that's promising—
It's Lady Liberty!
I may be crazy, but it seems
She's smiling down at me.

At last! I've finally found the place
To lay my anchor down.

Anchor to stay.
Anchor to stay.

(Fluke)

Wintertime

It's wintertime
And ten below
But I don't care
'Cause there is snow!

I've got my scarf,
I've got my sleigh,
And down this hill
I'll zoom away.

Prepare for launch.
Look out below!
Get ready, get set . . .
Three,
     Two,
        One . . .
GO!

(Jack Frost)

Sleepy Lullaby

Night-night. Sleep tight.
The moon is shining. Stars are bright.
It's time to curl up in your bed
And rest your little sleepy head.

Furry Facts

The Sweetheart

Life is sweet for **Poppie,** a junk-food junkie with an insatiable sweet tooth. She loves eating things that are sticky, gooey, or chewy and will play dead when offered anything that remotely resembles a vegetable.

Favorite song: "Lollipop"

Pet peeve: Dentists

What makes her tail wag: The sound of the ice cream truck

Secret fact: She always eats dessert before dinner.

The Escape Artist

No fence can confine **Skedaddle!** This freedom lover seems to magically disappear each time he is returned to his yard.

Favorite song: "On the Road Again"

Hero: Houdini

What makes his tail wag: Green lights

Secret fact: He always packs a lunch.

The Pal

Laberjack is the strong, silent type and leads a simple life among the pines. As a loyal friend to both man and dog, he is always there to lend a helping paw.

Favorite book: The Call of the Wild

Pet peeve: Show dogs

What makes his tail wag: A job well done

Secret fact: He plants one new tree every day.

The Klutz

If you hear a crash or a smash, chances are **Grace** is not too far behind. She may stumble and bumble through the day, but she's never afraid to try something new.

Favorite song: "Amazing Grace"

Dream job: Professional ballet dancer

What makes her tail wag: A soft place to land

Secret fact: She's never sprained an ankle.

The Diva

The world revolves around **Honey.** This pampered pooch's secretive past includes rumors of her once being a stray!

Favorite possession: Her Tiffany dog tags

Favorite saying: "Please fetch that for me."

What makes her tail wag: Biscuits at the Ritz

Secret fact: She refuses to walk and demands to be carried.

The Odd Couple

For **Moose** and **Mini** the saying "love is blind" takes on new meaning. This poor love-struck soul will do just about anything for a fleeting glance from true love high above.

Favorite song: "Can't Take My Eyes off You"

Favorite movie: Lady and the Tramp

What makes his tail wag: Eye contact

Secret fact: Moose is the small dog.

The Adventurers

Daring explorers **Lewie** and **Clark** will tackle any field, forest, or stream in their quest for coveted treasures.

Hero: Indiana Jones

Pet peeve: Ticks

What makes their tails wag: Merit badges

Secret fact: They once dug up a dinosaur bone!

The Rivals

Pip and **Squeak** are twins who bicker and battle over anything and everything. From chew toys to a prized bone, each wants what the other has and will go to any length to get it!

Favorite song: "My Way"

Favorite pastime: Yelping for attention

What makes their tails wag: Wishbones

Secret fact: They never go to bed angry.

The Pool Boy

Splash was once afraid of the water, but now he is an accomplished swimmer. In fact, he works weekends as a lifeguard at the kiddie pool!
Favorite phrase: "Last one in is a rotten egg!"
Hero: Aquaman
What makes his tail wag: A game of Marco Polo
Secret fact: He does one heck of a backstroke.

The Buddies

Pea's a chip off the ol' bark, and **Pa** couldn't be prouder. This father and son are so close, they even share the same fleas!
Favorite pastime: Playing fetch
Favorite food: PEAnuts and POPcorn
What makes their tails wag: The dog days of summer
Secret fact: Pea has a brother—but he's a mama's boy.

The Bookworm

Monte is a brilliant bookworm. Although he enjoys reading anything he can get his paws on, he prefers studying books on animal behavior.
Favorite food: Alphabet soup
Pet peeve: Misplaced library books
What makes his tail wag: The smell of fresh ink
Secret fact: He once took a class to become a Seeing Eye dog.

The Dude

Every day is golden for **Woody.** When he's not out hotdoggin' in the big surf on his long board, he can be found hanging loose on the sand, getting stoked for the next set of swells.
Favorite song: "Good Vibrations"
Pet peeve: Boogie-boarders
What makes his tail wag: Hula girls
Secret fact: He's from Iowa.

The Slob

Meet **Stinky**—lover of dirt, hater of soap. He'll do anything to avoid a bath and has dreams of winning the title of World's Dirtiest Dog.
Favorite food: Raw garlic
Favorite movie: The Dirty Dozen
What makes his tail wag: Chasing skunks
Secret fact: He's actually a yellow Lab.

The Traveler

Fluke is an old salt. Having spent his life aboard a sailing ship, he's had some amazing adventures on the high seas and enjoys sharing stories of his travels—especially over a bucket of bones.
Favorite food: Fresh fish
Favorite pastime: Rest and relaxation
What makes his tail wag: Raising the anchor
Secret fact: He's afraid of cats.

The Daredevil

Jack Frost is a thrill seeker who lives life on the edge. Fearless and free-spirited, he has sledded down some of the neighborhood's most dangerous slopes searching for the ultimate rush.
Favorite song: "Wipe Out"
Favorite quote: "I feel the need for speed!"
What makes his tail wag: Fresh powder
Secret fact: His sled is actually a garbage-can lid.

The Lazybones

It's been another exhausting day of snacking and napping for **Sleepy.** All this hard work has made her tired, and she's ready for some shut-eye—but not before some warm milk and cookies.
Hero: The sandman
Pet peeve: Early birds
What makes her tail wag: Bedtime stories
Secret fact: She once slept through her own birthday party.